Unearthing Secrets: The Gold Sovereign Discovery

The Forgotten Mining Shaft: Introduction to the Discovery
Beneath the old, rugged earth, a long-abandoned shaft holds secrets buried by time; miners once dared to delve deep into its dark embrace. The air inside the shaft was thick with the scents of damp earth and decaying wood, a reminder of the hard labor that had taken place within its depths centuries before. As the torchlight pierced the oppressive darkness, the ancient timbers groaned, protesting the intrusion of modern explorers. With each step forward, the sense of trepidation grew, for it was known that this forsaken place held more than mere echoes of the past. It held the promise of uncovering history's best-kept secrets, concealed amid the suffocating silence. The sound of digging filled the air as the expedition team unearthed fragments of long-forgotten tools, remnants of a time when men had toiled tirelessly in pursuit of something precious. And then, amidst the debris, a glint caught their eye—a small, weathered coin, bearing the unmistakable mark of a bygone empire. This inconspicuous relic, lost to the annals of time, would come to rewrite the course of history, unveiling an enigmatic chapter long concealed within the earth's embrace. It was a discovery that rippled through the passage of time, evoking more questions than answers among those who dared to attribute meaning to its significance. For within the dust and shadows of that desolate shaft lay the potential to unveil an ancient mystery—a mystery that held the power to challenge the very fabric of scholarly understanding and reshape the narrative of a forgotten era.

Dust and Echoes: Revealing the Coin Cache
The torchlight flickered as it danced against the walls of the abandoned shaft, casting long shadows that seemed to stretch and reach out like ghostly fingers. The air was thick with dust, and the sound of slow, deliberate footsteps echoed in the silence. Each footfall seemed to awaken ancient whispers from the encroaching darkness, as if the very walls held secrets waiting to be unearthed. As the intrepid explorers ventured deeper into the depths of the

mine, they could sense a palpable tension building, a sensation that hung heavy in the stale air. Every cautious step brought them closer to the elusive cache they sought, but it also drew them further into the labyrinthine heart of mystery that surrounded it. Amidst the debris and detritus of centuries past, glimmers of something precious caught their eyes. A single beam of light fell upon a collection of ancient coins, nestled within the earth like forgotten relics of a bygone era. The gold sovereigns, though tarnished and worn with time, seemed to emanate an aura of silent power, as if each coin held within its weathered edges an untold tale of wealth, glory, and perhaps even treachery. But as they cautiously collected the coins, a sense of foreboding crept over them. The discovery was not merely a testament to the opulence of a forgotten era, but a mirror reflecting the darker undercurrents of history. Whispers of betrayal, subterfuge, and unspoken alliances seemed to echo through the hollow chamber, awakening a poignant awareness of the tangled web of human ambition and greed. And as they emerged from the depths of the mine, the weight of their discovery pressed heavily upon them. The dusty air seemed to cling to their skin, a palpable reminder of the layers of secrecy that had shrouded the cache for so long. As the first light of dawn broke through the horizon, casting an ethereal glow upon the surface world, the explorers carried with them not just a trove of ancient coins, but the knowledge that their find would unearth far more than mere riches – it would unravel a legacy buried in dust and echoes, revealing the timeless allure and perilous depths of human desire.

Tarnished Legacy: Examining the Historical Implications

The excavation of the coin cache marked a pivotal moment for historians and archeologists alike. As the dust settled and the gleam of the gold sovereigns emerged from their age-old hiding place, it heralded a grim reminder of a tarnished legacy. Each coin told a story, not just of opulence and wealth, but also of exploitation, suffering, and the dark underbelly of history. The meticulous examination of the coins revealed intriguing details about the rulers and regimes that had minted them. Every scratch, every worn edge spoke volumes about the circulation of currency, trade routes, and the power dynamics of the time. The coins became more than mere artifacts; they were windows into the past, offering a unique perspective on the struggles and triumphs of generations long gone. As the historical implications unfolded, a sense of unease permeated the scholarly circles studying the find. Whispers of long-buried secrets and clandestine transactions hinted at a dangerous game that had once played out in the shadows of power. The slow-burn suspense gripped the researchers as they delved deeper into the significance of the coin cache. Gritty realism painted a stark picture of the lives intertwined with the gold sovereigns. Tales of laborers toiling in harsh conditions, harrowing journeys of traders seeking fortune, and the relentless ambition of monarchs hungry for control wove a tapestry of human struggle and sacrifice. The immersive historical detail brought to life the era of political intrigue, betrayal, and shifting allegiances, casting a haunting shadow over the present revelation. The tarnished legacy of the gold sovereigns cast a long shadow over the academic community, sparking debates and revelations that promised to rewrite established narratives. As the weight of history bore down upon the researchers, the implications of the discovery grew, setting the stage for an unfolding saga of ancient alliances and disputed legacies.

The Cipher Unveiled: Setting the Codebreaking Stage

Echoes of Ink and Quill: Unraveling the Old Manuscripts

Beneath layers of dust, the ancient texts revealed glimpses of hidden communication techniques used by the Tudor court, intertwined with personal annotations and peculiar diagrams. As the scholars pored over the brittle pages, a sense of gritty realism pervaded the room. The musty scent of aged parchment hung heavy in the air, mingling with the flickering light of oil lamps. Each carefully turned page held the promise of long-buried secrets, driving the sense of slow-burn suspense ever deeper. The weight of centuries seemed to press down on their shoulders, each word and symbol an immersive gateway to historical intricacies that sent shivers down their spines.

The Midnight Scholar: A Lantern's Glow over Anomalies

The dimly lit chamber cast eerie shadows as the lone scholar meticulously pored over weathered parchments by the glow of a flickering lantern. Every crease, every blotch, and every intricately penned symbol on the fragile manuscripts held within them the tantalizing promise of unlocking hidden mysteries. Dust motes danced in the air as the scholar furrowed his brow, deeply engrossed in the anomalies that seemed to defy comprehension. Each stroke of the quill appeared deliberate, yet concealed a truth waiting to be unfurled under the piercing scrutiny of the determined researcher. This relentless pursuit of deciphering enigmas wrought in ink had become an arduous obsession for the scholar, driven by an insatiable thirst for knowledge and a desire to unveil the secrets carefully cloaked within the cryptic texts. The faint scratching of the quill against the parchment was periodically punctuated by tense, contemplative pauses, evoking an aura of quiet intensity that permeated the stillness of the night. As the hours unwound like the intricate coils of an ancient tapestry, the dim light of the lantern waned, casting elongated shadows that loomed ominously across the cluttered desk. The scholar's mind remained gripped by the enigmatic anomalies, each one akin to a phantasmagorical specter teasing the edges of understanding. A hush descended upon the chamber, thick with anticipation and the weight of unspoken revelations hovering just beyond reach. With steady determination, the scholar meticulously scrutinized each anomaly, tracing the looping patterns and cryptic symbols that seemed to shift and morph with elusive intent. In the profound silence of the nocturnal sanctuary, the fluttering of a moth against the window pane formed a stark counterpoint to the scholar's sober contemplation. The swaying flame of the lantern cast dappled illumination, animating the archaic script and coaxing forth fleeting glimpses of meaning from the esoteric quagmire of antiquity. Like a solitary voyager navigating an unfathomable labyrinth, the scholar unraveled the convoluted threads of anomalies, exuding an aura of gritty perseverance in the face of ceaseless uncertainty. Thus, as the night waned into the embrace of dawn, the scholar remained entrenched in a slow-burn quest, fervently pursuing the revelation that lay concealed within the enigmatic tapestry of historical anomalies.

Unfolding Patterns: The Language Concealed in Shadows

The old manuscripts revealed little at first glance, their parchments weathered and stained, their ink fading with time. Yet, as the midnight scholar delved deeper, a glimmer of understanding began to emerge. In the flickering light of his lantern, he pored over the intricate patterns and symbols, each stroke of the quill bearing significance that lay dormant for centuries. As he immersed himself in the cryptic language, the slow-burn suspense of unraveling the hidden messages unfolded. The deciphering process was neither swift nor simple, demanding perseverance and a keen eye for detail. Every shadow on the parchment seemed to hold a secret, urging the scholar to uncover the truths concealed within. Gritty realism infused the scholar's efforts as he confronted the gritty reality of codebreaking – the frustration of dead-ends, the tantalizing hints of progress, and the gnawing uncertainty of whether he was on the right path. The immersive historical detail lent weight to each revelation, tracing the origins of the cryptic language back to the clandestine corridors of power in Tudor England. Layer by layer, the patterns emerged from the shadows, revealing a web of deceit and intrigue woven into the very fabric of the documents. The scholar found himself caught in a labyrinth of hidden meanings and double entendres, every twist and turn leading him further into the heart of a mystery that could shatter kingdoms. With bated breath, he followed the tendrils of the code, inexorably drawn into the web of historical enigma. As the secrets began to take shape, the air crackled with anticipation, the weight of centuries pressing down on his shoulders. Each breakthrough brought him closer to unlocking a truth that had been obscured by the veils of time, a truth that held the power to rewrite the annals of history. And so, amidst the dusty tomes and musty scent of antiquity, the scholar persisted, driven by an unyielding resolve to pierce through the veils of obscurity. With every painstaking revelation, the web of conspiracy tightened its grip, casting long shadows across the corridors of power. The language concealed within the shadows beckoned forth a world fraught with peril and possibility, a world where reality and illusion intertwined in a mosaic of enigmatic revelation.

Symbols and Secrets: Delving into Tudor Mysteries

The Enigmatic Tapestry: Reading the Tudor Symbols
In the heart of Tudor England, symbols were more than just adornments; they were clandestine messengers, intricately woven into the very fabric of everyday life. The tapestries adorning the grand halls of courtiers and nobles concealed a web of subtle cues and covert communications. As I ventured deeper into the labyrinthine corridors of power, the intricate threads depicted scenes of ostentatious feasting and chivalrous quests, yet hidden within this grandeur lay a symphony of secrets waiting to be deciphered. Each vibrant thread whispered tales of loyalty and treachery, veiling a world of political intrigue within the folds of luxurious artistry. Symbols of triumph and honor subtly morphed into subtle declarations of allegiance or defiance, their true meanings cloaked in the guise of splendor and opulence. It was a world where alliances were forged, and adversaries identified, through an ingenious symbology that resided not only in the adornment of high towers but also in the mundane objects that graced the domestic sphere. Ordinary objects carried far more depth than met the eye, each one transforming into a canvas for intricate messages, from the quill resting upon the writing desk to the ornate pommel of a dagger nestled in a sheath. The language of symbols transcended mere artwork and architecture, weaving its intricate tale across the entirety of Tudor society. This rich tapestry of meaning breathed life into every facet of existence, casting shadows that spanned the breadth of the kingdom. Within the folds of draping fabric and carved stone, the emblems of political factions etched themselves into this dynamic landscape, each vying for supremacy and survival amidst the shifting tides of power. Behind every seemingly innocuous motif lay an underlying message, an unspoken oath, or a silent threat. Unraveling these enigmas would shed light on the inner workings of a realm poised on the brink of change, exposing the raw truth beneath the veneer of feigned civility. The echoes of heraldic symbols resonated with gritty realism, a constant reminder of the

perilous underworld intertwining with the ostensible opulence of courtly life. These symbols held the tantalizing promise of unraveling the mysteries shrouding Tudor society, drawing me further into the slow-burn suspense of a world cloaked in timeless intrigue and complexity.

Ink and Omen: Secrets Beneath the Royal Scrolls

The dim candlelight flickered in the opulent chamber, casting eerie shadows on the aged parchments strewn across the imposing oak table. Each scroll held within its carefully preserved confines the weight of centuries, their faded ink telling tales of power, deceit, and intrigue. The air was heavy with the scent of parchment and age, the silence broken only by the rhythmic scratch of a quill against vellum. As I gingerly unfurled the first scroll, the intricate calligraphy leapt out from the page, beckoning me into the labyrinth of Tudor mysteries. Each stroke of the pen seemed to hold a whispered secret, an omen of the tumultuous times that had given birth to this cryptic communication. The parchment bore witness to a kingdom steeped in uncertainty, where allegiances were as fragile as soap bubbles and treachery lurked beneath the veneer of courtly grandeur. Amidst the delicate swirls of ink, I sought clues to the enigmatic symbols that had long confounded scholars and historians. Each symbol carried the weight of history, casting shadows of suspicion and revelation. Every stroke of the quill seemed to echo the turbulent pulse of Tudor England, where every word could wield the power of life or death. The scrolls whispered of clandestine meetings, shadowy alliances, and veiled threats, their faded letters a testament to the precarious dance of power amidst the Tudor court. With bated breath, I pored over each line, unraveling the tantalizing web of secrets woven within the royal scrolls. As the night wore on, the chamber echoed with the palpable sense of impending discovery, each revelation drawing me deeper into the heart of Tudor intrigue. The layers of deception peeled away, revealing glimpses of long-buried conspiracies and whispered counsel. Through the haze of time, the ink spoke of political maneuvering, religious fervor, and the relentless pursuit of power. The secrets concealed within the royal scrolls held the key to unraveling the cloak of enigma that shrouded the Tudor dynasty, offering a tantalizing glimpse into a world fraught with peril and ambition. As dawn broke over the horizon, my weary eyes remained fixed on the ancient parchments, their ink-stained secrets illuminating the murky depths of Tudor mysteries, beckoning me ever closer to the heart of the realm's clandestine past.

Whispers in the Walls: Echoes of Hidden Messages

The candlelight flickered, casting eerie shadows on the damp walls of the old Tudor chamber. As I traced my fingers along the cold stones, I could almost feel the weight of centuries of secrets pressing down upon me. This was a place where whispers lingered, where the walls held hidden messages waiting to be deciphered. The air was heavy with the scent of age and intrigue, as if the very essence of Tudor history had seeped into the mortar. I imagined the courtiers of long ago, huddled in clandestine discussions, their words carefully chosen to mask their true intentions. The tapestries, faded with time, seemed to ripple with the ghosts of plots and conspiracies. I turned my attention to the ornately carved oak paneling, running my hand over the intricate designs. Could it be that these walls bore witness to the coded communications of spies and informants? Each knot in the wood, every subtle carving, seemed to hold a story untold. As I leaned in closer, I could almost hear the furtive whispers that must have echoed through these halls. This was not simply a room; it was a confession booth for the secrets of the Tudor court. The layers of history were palpable, and it was as if the very fabric of time had been woven into the very structure of the walls. It was a puzzle waiting to be solved, a mystery begging to be unveiled. In the dim light, I spied an intricate pattern etched near the fireplace. I felt a surge of anticipation as I realized that this might be the key to unlocking the cryptic messages hidden within these walls. Piece by piece, I scrutinized the markings, allowing myself to become lost in the labyrinth of symbols. Each stroke of the chisel seemed to pulse with significance, and I was determined to uncover the truth they concealed. As midnight approached, the edges of the room seemed to blur, and I found myself immersed in the world of Tudor espionage. Every crack, every imperfection in the stonework hinted at a forgotten tale. The slow-burn suspense of unraveling these mysteries gripped me, compelling me to continue my exploration into the night. Finally, as the first light of dawn pierced through the tiny window, I felt a sense of revelation wash over me. I had unearthed a snippet of a message, a fragment of a greater puzzle. The gritty realism of Tudor life clashed with the intrigue of coded communication, creating a web of historical detail that pulled me deeper into its folds. The whispers in the walls had begun to yield their secrets, and I knew that I was only scratching the surface of a much larger enigma.

A Glimpse of Intrigue: Cryptography in the Court

Dark Corners: The Unseen Hands at Work

The royal court was a labyrinthine world, filled with hidden players manipulating affairs from the shadows. It was a web of intrigue, where whispered conversations and clandestine alliances held more power than public proclamations. At the apex of the social hierarchy, the monarch reigned supreme, but beneath the glittering surface of courtly splendor, other figures pulled strings with deft precision. High-ranking nobles vied for favor and influence, each maneuvering to secure their positions and further their agendas. Yet, it was not only the titled aristocracy who wielded power in these dark corners; those with connections to the church, the military, or the secretive underworld also held sway over the destiny of the realm. In such an environment, trust was a rare commodity and betrayal a constant threat. The slow-burn suspense of the court's underbelly lay in the constant tension between appearance and reality, as hidden motives skewed every interaction. Every whispered word held the potential for revelation or ruin, weaving a complex tapestry of deceit and ambition. As the protagonist delved deeper into these dark corners, they uncovered a world where loyalties were fickle and secrets carried lethal consequences. Beneath the opulent façade of the court, the immersive historical detail painted a vivid picture of the power struggles that shaped the fate of nations. Here, the gritty realism of political maneuvering clashed with the grandeur of the Tudor court, highlighting the stark contrast between appearance and truth. As the narrative unfolded, the reader was drawn into a world where danger lurked around every corner, and the unseen hands of influence could alter the course of history with a single whispered command.

Intercepting Whispers: The Language of Secret Messages

The corridors and chambers of the Tudor court were awash with whispered intrigue, where every hushed conversation held the potential for treachery or revelation. Master cryptographers like Robert Bannatyne honed their skills in the art of intercepting and deciphering secret messages that passed through the court. Their work was marked by a gritty realism, as they navigated the ever-present danger of clandestine plots lurking in the shadows. Each intercepted whisper was a puzzle waiting to be unraveled, a slow-burn suspense building as the mystery unfolded. Immersion into historical detail enriched their methods, drawing on the complex interplay of political and religious tensions that pervaded the era. The language of secret messages was an intricate tapestry, woven with symbols and codes designed to shield vital information from prying eyes. In pursuing these enigmatic missives, Bannatyne and his ilk delved deep into the psyche of the court, understanding the motivations and movements of its influential figures. In the dim glow of candlelit chambers, the cryptographers meticulously cataloged the intercepted whispers, pouring over every detail in search of patterns and clues. The tension in the air was palpable, as each decrypted message unveiled a fragment of the court's intricate web of deception. It was a dance of wits, a testament to the enduring allure of slow-burn suspense as they pieced together the clandestine machinations that threatened the stability of the realm. Their efforts mirrored the relentless march of history, where allegiances shifted like tides and hidden agendas lay buried beneath layers of political subterfuge. The immersive historical detail served as their compass, guiding them through the labyrinthine intrigues of the Tudor court. Through their tireless dedication, a greater truth began to emerge, shedding light on the perilous games played within the silent court, where loyalties hung by a delicate thread and trust was a scarce commodity.

The Silent Court: Navigating the Web of Deception

The candlelight cast eerie shadows upon the walls of the dimly lit chamber, as the courtiers circulated, each with a facade of poise and grace. Yet beneath their elegant demeanor lurked a labyrinth of deceit. The air was heavy with tension, the unspoken language of allegiances and treachery. A single misstep could lead to ruin, or worse, the chopping block. Amidst the opulent tapestries and gilded trinkets, whispers drifted like smoke, carrying tales of clandestine alliances and whispered confidences. Every gesture, every flicker of expression, held potential for interpretation, veiling the truth in layers of illusion. One false move amidst the treacherous dance of power within the court could unravel carefully laid plans, sparking a cascade of dire consequences. In this perilous arena, information was coveted currency, exchanged in coded missives and clandestine rendezvous. Only those who could navigate the intricate web of deception had any hope of unraveling the plots that threatened to upheave the fragile balance of the kingdom. The intricacies of cryptic messages intertwined seamlessly with the elaborate court etiquette, rendering the truth a scarce commodity amidst the intricate dance of falsehoods. Deep within the labyrinthine halls of the palace, agents and informants moved under shrouds of anonymity, their identities obscured by cloaks of discretion. Their loyalty, pledged in shadowed alcoves and secluded gardens, bound them to a covert world where loyalties could shift with the changing tides of ambition and fear. Each spoken word, each discreet nod, carried weighty implications that reverberated through the delicate fabric of royal intrigue, weaving a tapestry of deception that masked the true intentions of those who maneuvered within the silent court. Within this enigmatic realm, trust was a fragile commodity traded sparingly, for fear of the repercussions that might accompany misplaced faith. Allegiances were constantly in flux, alliances formed and broken in the subtle politics of survival and ascendancy. Forged letters, secret meetings, and elusive symbols concealed the agendas that simmered beneath the seemingly tranquil surface of courtly elegance, ensnaring all who dared to cross the invisible boundaries of loyalty and betrayal. As night descended over the labyrinthine corridors of power, the silent court continued its clandestine ballet, each unknown figure playing their part in a symphony of subterfuge, where even the staunchest of convictions could be swayed by honeyed promises and whispered half-truths. In the heart of the Machiavellian dance, the truth remained an elusive specter, shrouded by the deceptive waltz of the court's silent opera.

The Master's Apprentice: Learning the Language of Codes

Beneath the Master's Watchful Eye: An Induction into Shadows Under the dim glow of flickering candlelight, the young apprentice found themselves in a world shrouded in secrecy and the weight of responsibility. The master, a figure of commanding presence, regarded them with an unwavering gaze that seemed to pierce through the very soul. Each step, each whisper, carried untold significance in this clandestine realm, and the apprentice could feel the gravity of their journey taking hold. They soon realized that the complexities of espionage transcended mere words and gestures; it was a symphony of nuanced signals, silent glances, and meticulous arrangements. With each passing moment, the apprentice's initial trepidation metamorphosed into a profound respect for the master's exacting standards, for they began to comprehend the unyielding demands of this perilous world. The master, while taciturn, possessed an enigmatic quality that drew the apprentice deeper into the intricate web of subterfuge and intrigue. It was a world of duplicity and finesse, where every action had to be carefully weighed against unseen consequences. Their initiation into this shadowy realm unfolded gradually, with the master imparting inscrutable knowledge that stirred both fascination and apprehension in the apprentice's heart. Every lesson, every demonstration, seemed to reveal but a fraction of the cryptic lexicon of covert communication. As they delved deeper, the apprentice came to understand that in this art of concealment, nothing was arbitrary—all held coded meaning, waiting to be deciphered by those astute enough to discern the patterns amid the chaos. Beneath the master's watchful eye, the apprentice felt the weight of history bearing down upon them, intertwining their fate with the long lineage of clandestine messengers who had come before. It was a lonely yet captivating path, one that demanded unyielding dedication and an unshakeable resolve. In the stillness of the candlelit room, the apprentice's perception of the world shifted, giving way to a newfound understanding of the perilous dance they were now a part of—a dance poised on the edge of betrayal and revelation, concealed within the shadows of history.

Silent Lexicon: Crafting Codes in Candlelit Rooms

The candlelight flickered against the walls, casting long shadows across the dimly lit room. Here, amidst the secrecy and stillness, a silent lexicon seemed to come alive. The air was heavy with anticipation as I watched my master deftly inscribe intricate symbols onto parchment, each stroke deliberate and purposeful. The methodical nature of his movements revealed the artistry behind crafting codes, a skill honed through years of clandestine communication. With each delicate line and curve, he sculpted language into a form meant only for those initiated into its mysteries. As I observed, my senses heightened, attuned to the weight of every silence and the power held within each obscured meaning. The pause between breaths seemed charged with unspoken significance, as if the very act of exhaling could betray the secrets swirling in the room. Every scratch of quill on parchment echoed like a heartbeat, a rhythm that mirrored the pulse of our covert world. In these candlelit rooms, the boundaries between innocence and intrigue blurred, and the flickering flames bore witness to the birth of messages destined to never see the light of day. I felt the weight of responsibility settle upon my shoulders, the knowledge that I was now entrusted with the art of preserving and unraveling hidden truths. The thrill of wielding this silent lexicon mingled with the sobering awareness of the dangers lurking in the shadows, waiting to pounce on any careless misstep. It was here, in the hushed intimacy of this chamber, that I learned the true gravity of our work. Each cipher meticulously constructed carried with it the burden of lives hanging in the balance—secrets interlaced with survival. And in the depth of the night, with only the whisper of quill meeting parchment to accompany me, I understood that the journey ahead would demand more than mere skill or cunning. It would require an unwavering resolve and an intimacy with danger, a willingness to delve deeper into the murky waters of treachery and deceit. Through the alchemy of ink and ingenuity, we forged a shield of clandestine knowledge, one that both protected and endangered us all in equal measure.

Unseen Forces: The Art of Hidden Messages

As the apprentice delves deeper into the clandestine world of codebreaking, a heavy cloak of secrecy descends upon the chambers where these ghostly whispers echo. With each passing day, the young apprentice becomes well-versed in the art of concealing messages within innocuous letters and innocuous symbols. The stakes are unbearably high, and the slightest misstep could unleash unspeakable consequences. Every motion, every whisper is imbued with a palpable tension, as the realization dawns that their newfound skills carry grave significance in shaping the shadowy underbelly of Tudor intrigue. Each flickering candle casts elongated shadows across the parchment strewn tables, as the sage master imparts the intricacies of steganography – the concealment of information within the folds of innocuous communication. The air crackles with the intensity of unspoken truths, binding the apprentice to an ancient brotherhood that predates the courts of kings and queens.

Under the Gilded Roof: Spies Amongst the Courtiers

Veils of Deception: Hidden Agendas in the Royal Court
The royal court was a bewitching labyrinth of veiled intentions and palpable tension, where every echo was laden with secrets and every glance held the weight of unspoken alliances. Within these hallowed halls, power was not solely wielded by those with crowns or titles; it was also seized through clandestine whispers and subtle maneuvers. The courtiers navigated a treacherous dance, their every move orchestrated with meticulous calculation, for the stakes were high and the consequences dire. In this cauldron of intrigue, the hidden agendas of the courtiers veiled their true intentions, shrouding them in a cloak of ambiguity and uncertainty. Each feigned smile and whispered conversation concealed a myriad of motivations, from personal ambition to loyal devotion, and from clandestine loyalties to treacherous betrayals. As the flickering candlelight cast elongated shadows across the gilded walls, the air crackled with an undercurrent of betrayal, woven into the very fabric of courtly affairs. One could almost taste the tension that permeated the opulent chambers, as courtiers deftly navigated through the intricate web of social and political affiliations. Every gesture, every carefully chosen word, was laden with layers of implication, hinting at ploys and counter-plots that lay just beneath the surface. Amidst the finery and extravagance, one had to possess a keen eye to discern the subtle power plays and the whispered confidences exchanged behind jeweled fans and embroidered silks. However, beyond the façade of civility and decorum, a more primal struggle unfolded, driven by raw ambition and insatiable hunger for influence. Seething under the patina of propriety, the courtiers vied for favor and privilege, each maneuvering to build their own dominion within the intricate tapestry of courtly politics. Meanwhile, alliances shifted like sand dunes in a tempest, and loyalties were as fragile as spun glass. This clandestine game was no less dangerous than wars waged on open fields; here, victory meant securing a place at the monarch's side, while defeat

consigned one to ignominy and obscurity. As the shadows lengthened and the night cloaked the court in secrecy, the hidden agendas of the royal court were laid bare, revealing a complex tableau of veiled deceptions and obscured allegiances. It was within these dimly lit corridors, amidst the silken rustle of petticoats and the muted clink of goblets, that the true nature of courtly machinations came to light, drawing the unwary deeper into its enigmatic embrace.

Crimson Shadows: Betrayal Beneath the Golden Chandeliers

The opulent grandeur of the royal court belied the treacherous undercurrents that snaked through its gilded corridors. As dusk descended, casting elongated shadows across the marbled floors, the courtiers gathered for an evening of revelry and political maneuvering. Underneath the glittering chandeliers, their laughter and masked pleasantries concealed a network of deceit and thinly veiled threats. The flickering candlelight seemed to cast an eerie glow on the sly glances and clandestine whispers that permeated the air. Each movement spoke volumes as they navigated the intricate dance of alliances and betrayals. Amidst the decadent splendor, the grit of reality reared its head, reminding all present that survival in the court was contingent on guile and strategic finesse. Every ornate gesture carried weight, every carefully chosen word held the potential to be a death knell. The slow-burn suspense of impending betrayal hung heavy in the air, like a thick fog enveloping the unsuspecting prey. Behind the façade of perfumed elegance, the simmering tension threatened to boil over at any moment, drawing every soul deeper into the suffocating embrace of secrecy and danger. The claustrophobic ambiance added a palpable edge to the relentless game of political chess being played out in the heart of splendor. Each courtier became a player in this ruthless game, dancing delicately on the knife's edge, never quite sure who would emerge victorious in this deadly match of wits and hidden agendas. Beyond the dazzling veneer, shadows lurked, eager to consume the unsuspecting or the ill-prepared. Within these hallowed halls, loyalty was a scarce commodity, easily traded or discarded in pursuit of personal gain. The echoes of past betrayals reverberated through each passing moment, a constant reminder of the unforgiving nature of court politics. It was amidst this shimmering facade that the true savagery of human ambition was laid bare, entwined with the captivating aroma of power and privilege. The crimson shadows whispered tales of greed, envy, and treachery, painting a stark portrait of the price exacted by those who danced beneath the golden chandeliers.

The Silent Chamber: Unmasking the Elusive Informants

The courtiers of Tudor England moved in a delicate dance of alliances and espionage, their every word and action scrutinized beneath the gilded roof of power. Within the silent chamber, where whispered secrets echoed against the tapestries and flickering flames cast shadows of suspicion, the elusive informants thrived. Their allegiances were masked behind smiles and courtesies, each exchange laden with double meanings and concealed intentions. In this world of subterfuge, Lady Margaret, a trusted confidante to the Queen, sought to unravel the web of deceit that enshrouded the court. Her keen eyes missed nothing, and she made it her mission to expose the informants who lurked within the hallowed halls of power. Yet, every revelation only led to deeper layers of intrigue, as whispers hinted at informants within her inner circle, casting doubt upon even the most loyal attendants. As the days turned into weeks, and the weeks bled into months, the slow-burn suspense of uncovering these informants tested Lady Margaret's resolve. Each conversation, each exchange of glances, carried the weight of uncertainty, each step forward threatened by the fear of an unseen betrayal. The gritty realism of the court's treacherous landscape became palpable, the air heavy with the scent of duplicity and the clinking of hidden agendas. Immersive historical detail colored every interaction within the silent chamber, depicting the intricacies of Tudor courtly life. From the elaborate tapestries adorning the walls to the meticulous arrangement of goblets on the banquet table, every element spoke volumes about the opulence and artifice that shrouded the pursuit of power. The readers could almost feel the tension in the air, taste the anticipation tinged with apprehension, as Lady Margaret navigated the treacherous terrain of court politics in her relentless quest to unmask the elusive informants. And so, within the silent chamber, the stakes rose higher with each passing day, fraught with the harrowing knowledge that a single misstep could lead to ruin. The reader was drawn deeper into the carefully constructed world of Tudor intrigue, lingering on the precipice of discovery alongside Lady Margaret, yearning for resolution amidst the dizzying array of characters and their labyrinthine machinations.

Shadows in the Gallery: Engaging the Intelligence Network

Portraits in Shadows: Infiltrating the Web of Deception
Within the opulent halls of the royal court, the protagonist delves into the intricate web of deception that shrouds the clandestine activities of spies. As he navigates the dimly lit corridors and secret passages, subtle whispers and furtive glances hint at the presence of hidden agendas. Gritty realism is palpable in the air, as every shadow seems to harbor a potential informant or double agent. The protagonist's senses are heightened, attuned to the slightest movements and cryptic exchanges that permeate the atmosphere of suspicion. Slow-burn suspense builds as he pieces together the fragments of information, realizing that the artful dance of deceit extends far beyond the polished veneer of courtly etiquette. Immersive historical detail brings to life the intricacies of communication in an era where trust was a rare currency and treachery lurked behind every tapestry. The protagonist studies the portraits lining the gallery walls, recognizing that each brushstroke conceals more than just the visage of a noble. These paintings are windows into the covert channels used by spies, conveying coded messages through enigmatic symbolism and subtle gestures. The protagonist deciphers the hidden meanings within the haunting gazes and enigmatic smiles, unraveling the threads that bind together this clandestine network. Every stroke of the brush becomes a clue, every imperfection a deliberate signal. Amidst the grandeur of the court, the protagonist finds himself immersed in a world of calculated subterfuge and perilous alliances. Secrets lie in plain sight, concealed within the strokes of a painter's brush and the glint of a jeweled brooch. With each revelation, the stakes heighten, and the tangled web of deception tightens its grip. The protagonist becomes entangled in this labyrinth of intrigue, realizing that to survive in this treacherous landscape, one must master the art of subterfuge and outwit those who dwell in the shadows.
Echoes of Betrayal: Mapping the Threads of Intelligence

The air hung heavy with the weight of knowledge and the burden of distrust. In the dimly lit chambers, where whispers were exchanged like precious commodities, the echoes of betrayal reverberated through the corridors of power. Every footstep seemed to carry the weight of a thousand secrets, the sound muffled by centuries of intrigue. As I delved deeper into the labyrinth of espionage, the threads of intelligence unraveled before me like a tapestry of deceit. Each informant, each double agent, wove a complex web of half-truths and hidden agendas, blurring the line between loyalty and betrayal. The faces that once bore the illusion of trust now appeared as mere masks, concealing the true intentions of those who prowled in the shadows. In the hallowed halls adorned with priceless art, I observed the subtle gestures and fleeting glances that spoke volumes in their silence. The portraits of revered ancestors gazed down upon us, bearing witness to the clandestine exchanges that played out beneath their watchful eyes. It was here, amidst the masterpieces of a bygone era, that I began to discern the patterns of subterfuge that had eluded me thus far. The slow-burn suspense of this clandestine dance was palpable, the tension thickening with each passing moment. I could almost taste the bitter tang of duplicity, a flavor that lingered in the air like an unspoken accusation. Every step I took, every conversation I overheard, added another thread to the intricate tapestry that was woven from the fabric of deception. As the pieces of the puzzle fell into place, I found myself confronting the harsh reality of my own naivety. The allies I had trusted implicitly now cast sinister shadows, their allegiance swayed by the allure of power and the promise of riches. Yet, amidst the sea of treachery, a few beacons of integrity emerged— individuals whose unwavering dedication to the cause reminded me that honor still thrived in the heart of darkness. With meticulous precision, I began to map out the convoluted networks of information exchange, tracing the pathways that led to the heart of the intelligence apparatus. Each node represented a potential source of revelation, a conduit through which the truth could be distilled from the murky waters of deception. But with each discovery came the realization that the intricacies of espionage defied simple comprehension; it was a realm where loyalties shifted like shifting sands, and allegiances were as transient as the changing tides. Yet, armed with the knowledge of the interconnected strands of betrayal and loyalty, I stood at the precipice of uncovering the ultimate truth. For within the shadows of the gallery, where portraits whispered of forgotten intrigues, I sought to unravel the enigma of the pact that bound together the architects of deception.

Silent Agreements: Crafting the Pact of Secrets

As the cold moon cast its pale glow over the ancient cobblestones, a hushed conspiracy unfolded in the dimly lit chamber. The flickering candlelight danced across the faces of those gathered in secrecy, their eyes reflecting a mixture of determination and trepidation. Each participant bore the weight of their hidden allegiances, bound by a silent pact woven from whispers and veiled intentions. Their breath hung in the air, heavy with the unspoken burden of knowledge that could topple empires and seal fates. This was the crucible where the fate of nations lay, and the air crackled with an electric undercurrent of raw ambition and calculated risk. In the shadows, a careful dance of power played out, orchestrated by those who wielded information as deftly as a swordsman wields his blade. The stakes were high, and the carefully calibrated balance of trust and betrayal teetered on the edge of oblivion. Every step was a delicate maneuver, threading the needle of opportunity while avoiding the entangling web of deceit that threatened to ensnare them all. Amidst the echoes of cannon fire and the scent of gunpowder that lingered in the air, the clandestine figures forged an unspoken alliance, binding themselves to a code of silence that transcended loyalties and ambitions. Words held the power to condemn or redeem, and each syllable uttered in the chamber resonated with the weight of destinies yet to unfold. As parchments bearing cryptic symbols exchanged hands, the intricate dance of espionage wove a tapestry of intrigue, blurring the lines between friend and foe. The veil of secrecy shrouded the truth, and within its enigmatic folds, the participants pledged their unwavering allegiance to the clandestine cause that threaded through the corridors of power and influence. The silence hummed with tension, punctuated only by the occasional creak of floorboards and the soft rustle of fabric as whispered confidences passed from one conspirator to another. Shadows flickered and swayed, mirroring the intricate machinations at play. With unflinching resolve, the conspirators faced the perilous path ahead, driven by an unyielding determination to safeguard their clandestine alliance. Every gesture, every fleeting glance, carried the weight of unspoken oaths sworn in the crucible of adversity. The murky depths of political intrigue beckoned, drawing the participants deeper into the treacherous labyrinth of subterfuge and clandestine accord. Forged in fire and tempered by the crucible, the pact of secrets bound them together in a fragile yet unbreakable bond, poised to shape the destiny of nations and rewrite the annals of history.

Whispers from the Confessional: Understanding Catholic Motivations

Echoes of Faith: Murmurs in the Dark

Amidst the flickering candlelight and hushed murmurs, the confessional becomes a clandestine haven for desperate souls seeking absolution. Here, within the dim recesses of the confessional booth, the weight of faith intertwines with the burden of secrecy, igniting a palpable tension that lurks beneath the surface of devotion. The air hangs heavy with the weight of suppressed confessions and solemn vows, as the faithful embark on a treacherous journey through the labyrinth of their own consciences. Whispers flutter like fragile moths in the dark, weaving a tapestry of loyalties and betrayals that threaten to unravel at the slightest provocation. Those who seek solace in the confessional tread a precarious path, navigating the perilous terrain of hidden truths and veiled motives. Each whispered confession is a thread in the tangled web of secrecy, bound by a code of silence that fractures under the strain of conflicting allegiances. The sanctity of the confessional is besieged by the turmoil of a kingdom torn asunder by religious strife, casting a long shadow over the soul-searching conversations that unfold within its walls. As fervent believers grapple with their inner demons, the confessional becomes an arena where whispered grievances and unspoken resentments converge, threatening to rupture the fragile peace that cloaks the realm. Charting a course through this treacherous landscape requires a keen understanding of the clandestine dance of secrets and sins that permeates every whispered exchange. The echoes of faith reverberate against the stone walls, carrying with them the weight of unspoken fears and fervent convictions. Behind each penitent's whispered confession lies a woven fabric of unyielding loyalties and profound internal conflicts, each strand poised to unravel at the most inopportune moment. As the foundation of the kingdom trembles under the weight of religious division, the shadows cast by the confessional grow longer, harboring the simmering tensions that threaten to erupt into open conflict. In this murky milieu of murmurings and muffled soliloquies, the seeds of discord take root, entwined with the eternal struggle between faith and faction. Amidst the suffocating embrace of the confessional, loyalities are tested, and the stage is set for a slow-burn suspense that promises to engulf a kingdom on the brink of upheaval.

The Confessor's Dilemma: Secrets and Sin

The confessional offered a sanctuary for whispered confidences, a place where hidden truths and the weight of sin intertwined within the stone walls. Every creak of the wooden divider seemed to echo with the struggles of the faithful, their burden laid bare before the priest. The flickering candlelight cast shadows upon anguished faces, perpetuating an atmosphere rife with palpable tension. As the faithful sought absolution, the confessor was confronted with a precarious web of secrets and sins. Each whispered revelation unraveled another layer of human frailty and moral conflict, drawing the confessor deeper into the intricate tapestry of human nature. With each confession, the confessor bore witness to the clandestine motives that drove the devout to acts both virtuous and damning. The confessor's own conscience became entwined with the burdens of others, grappling with the weight of shared transgressions and the dilemma of preserving the sanctity of the confessional seal. Intimate revelations sparked a slow-burn suspense, as the confessor navigated the treacherous terrain of safeguarding trust while wrestling with the knowledge of unspeakable deeds committed in blind devotion. Meanwhile, amidst the swirling incense and murmured prayers, the confessor channeled gritty realism in understanding the stark realities of faith and human fallibility. The confessional became a stage for the raw emotions and unyielding conflicts that resided within the hearts of the faithful, offering a glimpse into their innermost struggles as devout Catholics wrestling with their conscience. Within this immersive historical detail, the confessional bore witness to the cloak-and-dagger intrigues that lurked beneath the veneer of religious devotion—a clandestine world where political aspirations and religious motivations converged, weaving an intricate tapestry of loyalty, betrayal, and sacrificial penance.

Through the confessor's ears, a mosaic of Catholic motivations emerged, each colored by the turbulent backdrop of a kingdom torn between faiths. The Confessor's Dilemma burgeoned, laden with the weight of collective confessions and mortal dilemmas that tested the very fabric of belief and conviction, casting a spell of introspection and intrigue over the sacred enclave betwixt shadow and light.

Threads of Devotion: The Tug of Loyalty

The tangled web of loyalties within the Catholic community was a testament to the intricate nature of faith and politics intertwined. As clandestine gatherings convened in dimly lit chambers, fervent whispers punctuated the air as devotees grappled with the pressures of aligning with their religious beliefs against the backdrop of political turbulence. Each individual bore the weight of their convictions, knowing that any misstep could lead to dire consequences. Amidst this struggle, a palpable tension thrummed through the congregation, binding them together in an unspoken understanding of the risks they all faced. The tug of loyalty was undeniable, pulling them closer to their faith while simultaneously entwining them further into the perilous machinations of the divided realm. In the silence of confession, the burdens of allegiance and treachery lay heavy on the hearts of those who sought solace within the sanctity of the confessional. The faint glimmer of candlelight danced across faces etched with conflict, illuminating the anguish that accompanied their unwavering dedication to their cause. Each whispered revelation held the potential to shift the balance of power, creating a haunting undercurrent of suspense that left every soul within the confines of the confessional wrought with a sense of impending upheaval. Unbeknownst to them, the threads of devotion they clung to were intricately woven into a tapestry of secrecy and betrayal, each strand holding the fate of lives in its delicate embrace. This intricate dance of allegiances and obligations added layers of complexity to an already turbulent era, where the slow-burn suspense of clandestine meetings shaped the destinies of both devout individuals and the very fabric of history itself. The labyrinthine paths of loyalty and faith converged in these moments, leaving an indelible mark on those who navigated the perilous journey, forever bound by the enduring threads of devotion.

Webs of Deceit: Navigating Political Treachery

The Intrigue Beneath: Hidden Agendas in the Halls of Power
In the hallowed halls of power, where the clashing ambitions of nobles and courtiers intertwine with the fates of a kingdom, political rivalries simmer like a cauldron of treachery. Each step is fraught with the tension of subterfuge and clandestine maneuvers, as the very foundation of the throne's stability is tested by hidden agendas. The court, a labyrinthine tapestry of conflicting interests, is a breeding ground for whispered betrayals and deceitful alliances, each thread carefully woven to either uphold or unravel the delicate fabric of influence and power. Amidst this intricate dance of intrigue, double agents slink through the shadowed corridors, their loyalties shrouded in ambiguity and their whispered words laden with enigmatic intent. Their silhouettes cast against the flickering torchlight serve as a chilling reminder of the ever-present threat of espionage, threading its tendrils through the heart of the court. No individual can be trusted implicitly, and every exchange harbors the potential for a subtle knife thrust in the dark. The air hums with anticipation as the acrid scent of fear mingles with the heady perfume of ambition, manifesting as an almost tangible specter that envelops the court in an atmosphere of perpetual apprehension. Rumors swirl like ethereal phantoms, their presence pervasive but their truths often obscured by layers of artifice. Whispers beneath echoing arches carry the weight of unspoken secrets, each syllable bearing the weight of potential revelation or ruin. Beneath the veneer of grandeur and opulence, a web of concealed motives and ill-concealed venality thrives. With feigned smiles and polished courtly grace, the nobles engage in a shadowed ballet of cunning manipulation, wary eyes perpetually scanning for the telltale signs of duplicity. It is a theater of power plays and subtle stratagems, where every move is calculated and every word is laced with subtext, a terrain where survival hinges upon recognizing the veiled blades poised to strike. Here, amidst courtly pomp and lavish indulgence, lies the

seething undercurrent of political ambition, propelled by the currents of influence and the ceaseless pursuit of dominance. The struggle for supremacy wages beneath gilded ceilings and amidst sumptuous banquets, mirroring the precarious balance that holds the realm in thrall. In this perilous arena of power, the stakes are nothing less than the future of the kingdom itself, a confluence of history and personal ambition that intertwines fate with the actions and machinations of calculating minds.

A Dance of Shadows: Espionage and Double Agents

The Tudor court is a stage for covert maneuvers, where every smile harbors secrets and every word carries hidden intent. Espionage weaves its tangled web through the gilded chambers and dimly lit corridors, as double agents ply their trade under the guise of loyalty. The faint rustle of silk disguises the murmur of clandestine exchanges, and the gleam of a dagger is concealed beneath a gloved hand. Informants flit like phantoms through the court, trading in whispers and favors, slipping cryptic missives between allies and adversaries alike. Loyalties shift like shadows, as each noble vies for advantage, feigning devotion to the crown while nurturing ambitions that threaten to upend the delicate balance of power. Amidst the opulent masques and sumptuous banquets, masked figures move with grace and guile, concealing their true purpose behind elaborate facades. Behind closed doors, coded letters change hands, carrying the weight of treachery and deceit. Spies weave through the dance of diplomacy, their steps measured and calculated, their allegiance a fluid thing that shifts with the wind. The thrill of espionage infuses the air with tension, the slow burn of suspense kindling beneath the surface of Courtly decorum. Each gesture becomes a calculated risk, every whispered confidence a potential trap as the players in this deadly game navigate the treacherous landscape of political ambition. Secrets lie buried beneath layers of intrigue, waiting to be unearthed by those bold enough to delve into the heart of the shadows. Yet amidst the perilous dance of spies and deceivers, alliances are forged in the crucible of danger, and trust blooms in the unlikeliest of hearts. Amidst the grim reality of betrayal and deception, the flicker of camaraderie offers a glimmer of hope, drawing disparate souls together in pursuit of a common cause.

As the stakes grow higher and the threats more imminent, the tension mounts, promising a gripping tale of subterfuge and revelation.

The Serpent's Tongue: False Promises and Dangerous Alliances

The court was a tangled web of deceit, spun by lies whispered in the shadows and false promises that bound men to treacherous alliances. As the master of the spy network, it was my duty to navigate these dangerous waters with steely resolve and unyielding determination. The air was thick with tension, every word and glance laden with hidden agendas and dangerous intentions. In the dimly lit chambers, nobles spoke in hushed tones, striking deals that sealed fates and sowed discord. I observed, always vigilant, deciphering the nuances of their conversations, identifying the threads of deceit that wove through the tapestry of the court. Freedoms were bartered, loyalties tested, and treachery lurked in the most unexpected places. Each step was fraught with peril, every decision weighed against the backdrop of political intrigue and personal ambition. The seductive lure of power clouded judgment, blurring the line between friend and foe. Trust became a precious commodity, bought and sold like a rare jewel, and even the closest confidants concealed ulterior motives behind charming smiles and honeyed words. It was a deadly game, where allegiances shifted like sand dunes in a desert storm, and one misstep could lead to irreversible consequences. Yet, amidst the labyrinth of deceit, a glimmer of hope remained. For within the heart of darkness, flickered the light of truth, a beacon that guided me through the murky depths of betrayal and manipulation. Uncovering the web of lies required patience and keen insight, for beneath the mask of civility lay the fangs of duplicity, ready to strike at the slightest vulnerability. With each revelation, the intricate patterns of deception unraveled, exposing the sinister underbelly of nobility and the festering sores of greed and ambition. I navigated this treacherous landscape with unwavering determination, knowing that the price of failure was far greater than the burden of secrecy. The serpentine dance of false promises and dangerous alliances tested my resilience, but I stood unyielding, a sentinel against the encroaching darkness.

Allies and Adversaries: Trust Within the Court

Whispers in the Corridors: Unease Amongst the Courtiers
The candlelit corridors of the Tudor court were cloaked in an air of apprehension, where every whisper seemed to echo with the weight of impending treachery. Courtiers moved with measured steps, their gazes wary as they exchanged furtive glances and guarded conversations. Each rustle of silk and hushed murmur held the potential for concealed agendas and veiled alliances, weaving a tangled web of suspicion that permeated the very fabric of courtly life. The once-refined air now carried the scent of unease, mingling with the heady perfume of ambition and fear. In this simmering environment, loyalties wavered as allegiances were tested behind smiles and courteous nods, giving rise to a relentless undercurrent of doubt and uncertainty. With each passing day, the court resembled a stage for a clandestine play, where every player hid their true intentions behind a meticulously crafted facade. Secretive meetings took place in shadowed alcoves and dimly lit chambers, attended by figures draped in secrecy, their eyes alight with concealed motives that remained shrouded from prying eyes. It was within these clandestine gatherings that the balance of power shifted, as alliances formed and fractured in a delicate dance of treachery and deceit. The once-grand tapestries that adorned the walls seemed to absorb the whispered confidences and muted conspiracies, bearing witness to the veiled tensions that threaded through the court like an unseen thread. As the tension mounted, even the flicker of a torch seemed to cast elongated shadows that mirrored the doubts haunting the hearts of courtiers. It was amidst this gritty realism that the slow-burn suspense of suspicion and betrayal unfurled, casting an immersive historical detail that rendered the very essence of court intrigue in vivid, palpable hues.
Betrayal's Threshold: Testing the Bonds of Loyalty
The flickering candlelight cast eerie shadows on the dimly lit walls of the council chambers, as the air hung heavy with tension.

Whispers of discontent echoed through the room, a subtle undercurrent that hinted at deep-seated rifts within the court. Lord Wellesley, his stern countenance set in stone, surveyed the gathered nobles with a practiced gaze that betrayed none of the turmoil churning within him. The recent events had set in motion a dangerous game of power and politics, where alliances were tested and loyalties strained to their limits. As each noble vied for favor and influence, the once unshakable bonds of camaraderie were now fraying at the edges. Behind every courteous smile and feigned gesture of respect lurked treachery and deceit, as rival factions maneuvered for supremacy amidst the intricate web of courtly intrigue. The scent of betrayal hung in the air, a palpable presence that set nerves on edge and sowed seeds of doubt within even the closest confidants. In this ruthless pursuit of power, no one could be trusted, and the loyalty that once bound men together now felt as brittle as parchments left in the unforgiving hands of time. It was a perilous dance, where one misstep could lead to irreparable consequences, and the ever-present specter of betrayal loomed like a shadow over every whispered exchange and knowing glance. As the political machinations of the court unfurled with meticulous precision, allegiances were tested to their breaking point, and the true nature of trust within the hallowed halls of power became a precarious tightrope walk between survival and ruin. Hands clasped together in strained unity concealed minds fraught with suspicion, and the once noble pursuit of loyalty had devolved into a high-stakes gamble for survival. Each subtle maneuver and artful deception shifted the delicate balance of power, as adversaries sought to exploit the chinks in each other's armor and lay bare the vulnerabilities that lay hidden beneath the veneer of civility. The insidious game of betrayal had set the court ablaze with uncertainty, as erstwhile allies turned into foes and the battle lines of an unseen war were drawn in the sand. All the while, the looming threat of exposure and disgrace kept hearts racing and minds sharpened, casting a cloak of dread over the courtiers who dared to navigate the treacherous waters of intrigue and ambition.

The Silent Watchers: Unmasking Hidden Eyes

The corridors of power are always teeming with whispers and secrets, but in the court of Tudor England, these murmurs took on a life of their own. Allegiances were fragile, and loyalties could shift as swiftly as the wind. As the tension within the court grew palpable, a pervasive sense of paranoia settled over the courtiers, each eyeing the other with suspicion and wariness. Amidst this atmosphere of distrust, hidden eyes seemed to lurk in every shadow, their gaze unrelenting and inscrutable. Those who navigated the treacherous waters of court politics knew that they were never truly alone, always under the watchful eyes of both friend and foe. Whether it was the calculating glance of a rival or the furtive scrutiny of an unknown informant, the feeling of being observed became an ever-present weight upon their shoulders. Rumors abounded of secret meetings in dimly lit chambers, clandestine alliances forged in hushed tones, and missives passed surreptitiously from hand to hand. In such an environment, trust became a rare and precious commodity, guarded closely by those who understood its true value. Yet even the shrewdest courtiers could not escape the disquieting knowledge that their most intimate confidants might harbor ulterior motives. The walls appeared to have ears, and every murmur carried the potential for betrayal. With each passing day, the slow-burn suspense of courtly life intensified, steady and relentless like the ticking of a concealed timepiece. The specter of unseen adversaries cast a long shadow over the once glittering court, rendering every smile, every word, and every gesture into a potential maneuver in a dangerous game of political chess. nThe prospect of unmasking the hidden eyes that lurked in the court became an obsession for some, a puzzle to be unraveled at any cost. Yet, as the threads of suspicion tangled and twisted, separating truth from deception grew increasingly elusive. The silent watchers remained just beyond reach, their identities cloaked in the enigmatic shroud of secrecy. For the courtiers embroiled in this web of intrigue, the realization dawned that only by understanding the motivations and machinations of those around them could they hope to survive in this perilous domain. The pursuit of uncovering the truth behind the hidden eyes became not merely a matter of self-preservation, but a testament to their resilience in a world where trust was a precious rarity amid the grim realities of courtly life in Tudor England.

An Ill Wind: Hints of a Deadly Plot

The Stirring of Silence: Eavesdropping in the Hushed Chambers Court walls whisper of discontent as tensions rise among nobles. A careful observer may notice the clandestine meetings in dimly lit corridors, where words are spoken in hushed tones and furtive glances are exchanged. The air is thick with intrigue, each exhale a veiled threat, each silence pregnant with unspoken treachery. As shadows dance across the stone floors, eavesdroppers linger in the shadows, straining to catch morsels of conversation that may unravel the intricate web of deception. Within the chambers, voices fade into murmurs behind closed doors, their true intentions obscured by layers of subterfuge. Servants move about with practiced nonchalance, yet their eyes betray a keen awareness of the undercurrents of unease. It is amidst this atmosphere of uncertainty that alliances are forged and broken, secrets exchanged like currency in the dark corners of power. Amidst the flickering candlelight, figures move in silent collusion, their hands passing parcels and missives that bear the weight of unseen consequences. Every rustle of fabric, every creak of floorboards, speaks volumes in the symphony of suspicion that permeates the court. No detail is too trivial, no gesture too insignificant, as the players in this game of duplicity maneuver to safeguard their positions or secure their ambitions. From behind tapestried walls, muffled voices echo, revealing glimpses of hidden agendas and whispered dissent. Trust becomes an increasingly rare commodity, exchanged sparingly and often with a heavy price. Each exchange, laden with double entendre and layered meanings, carries the potential to tip the delicate balance of power in unforeseen directions, plunging the court into further disarray or heralding the unleashing of long-contained hostilities. In the susurrus of whispers, rumors take on a life of their own, weaving themselves into the very fabric of courtly existence. Every word becomes a weapon, every silence a prelude to revelation or ruin. The unraveling of schemes and the sustenance of alliances hinge upon the ability to discern the truth from the artifice, to navigate the labyrinth of deceit with unwavering resolve amidst the rising tide of suspicion. As the night draws its shroud over the court, the palpable tension lingers in the air like an ill omen, foreshadowing the storm that looms on the horizon and hinting at the inexorable collision of ambitions and agendas in the heart of power.

Veiled Transactions: Espials and Their Mysterious Messages

The air in the dimly lit chamber hung heavy with the scent of intrigue as clandestine transactions unfolded under the guise of innocent conversations. Cloaked figures leaned in close, their whispers barely audible above the crackling of the fireplace. The flickering flames cast eerie shadows on the walls, adding to the air of mystery that permeated the room. Amidst the seemingly casual exchanges, sharp-eyed observers would have noted the subtle gestures and exchanged glances that conveyed volumes in mere seconds. Every movement, every word was laden with hidden meaning, like a carefully crafted code waiting to be deciphered. Espials, skilled in the art of clandestine observation, moved with the stealth of shadows, their keen senses attuned to the slightest shifts in atmosphere. As the tension in the room ebbed and flowed, they watched, absorbing every detail like sponges. No whispered conversation or exchanged token escaped their notice, for within the delicate dance of words and movements lay the clandestine threads of an intricate web of deceit and treachery. The parchment that changed hands bore cryptic symbols and coded messages, its contents known only to the select few who wielded the power of knowledge. Each stroke of the quill conveyed the weight of empires, the fate of nations, and the destinies of those enmeshed in the web of political convolutions. As the night deepened, the conspiratorial symphony continued to play out. Every exchange, every veiled transaction added another layer to the tapestry of secrets and lies that blanketed the court. For behind the thin veneer of civility and protocol, the undercurrent of danger pulsed steadily, threatening to engulf all who dared to tread the perilous paths of power and ambition. In the flickering candlelight, the players in this deadly game remained locked in a silent ballet of deceit, their every move orchestrated to advance their own agendas while ensuring the downfall of their rivals. With each passing moment, the web drew tighter, entangling both the virtuous and the conniving in its gossamer embrace, leaving no soul untouched by the tendrils of suspicion and duplicity.

The Scent of Betrayal: An Unexpected Confession

The flickering candlelight cast wavering shadows across the musty chamber, as the air hung heavy with trepidation. At the center of the room, a lone figure knelt before the confession booth, their shoulders hunched in weary resignation. The hooded silhouette of the confessor, hidden in the alcove, exuded an aura of solemn authority as they listened intently to the whispered revelations. Time seemed to stand still within the confines of the confessional, punctuated only by the murmured admissions that tumbled forth like weighted stones. Each clandestine revelation carried the weight of centuries-old secrets, betrayals, and desperate loyalties that had festered in the heart of the court. The low drone of the voice behind the screen provided a haunting backdrop against which the sins of ambition, subterfuge, and deception were laid bare. From the depths of the dimly-lit confessional, the truth unfurled like a venomous bloom, weaving a tapestry of betrayal that spanned across courtly allegiances. The power struggle that simmered beneath the polished veneer of the royal court was exposed in all its gritty realism, illuminating the seething undercurrent of slow-burn suspense that had gripped the murky corridors of influence. As the confession wore on, the delicate balance of trust and betrayal within the court revealed itself in intricate detail. Whispers of covert alliances and concealed agendas seeped through the confessional grating, compelling the confessor to hold their breath in anticipation of the next damning revelation. The weight of historical intricacies bore down upon the intertwined lives of courtiers, swirling with the pervasive aroma of political upheaval and tantalizing intrigue. In this solemn enclave of whispered confessions, the pungent scent of betrayal permeated the air, lingering palpably as each revelation gnawed at the foundations of allegiance and honor. The web of deceit that ensnared the unsuspecting denizens of the court was woven with threads of haunting authenticity, capturing the essence of immersive historical detail in every whispered breath that spiraled upwards, carrying the harrowing testimonies to the archaic ceiling above. The unexpected confession rippled through the labyrinthine corridors of power, casting a foreboding shadow over the once pristine facade of loyalty and devotion. It echoed with the weight of unspoken truths and veiled machinations, heralding the impending storm of reckoning that loomed on the horizon, threatening to engulf the court in its tempestuous embrace.

Threads of Gold: A Numismatic Trail

Gleaming Treasures: The Gold Sovereign's Trail
In the dimly lit confines of the royal treasury, amidst the heavy scent of wax and aged parchment, a sense of foreboding hung in the air as we set out to trace the elusive trail of the gold sovereigns. These gleaming treasures held more weight than mere currency; they were symbols of power, coveted by monarchs and merchants alike for their undeniable authority and economic influence. Each coin bore the mark of its reign, a testament to the ever-shifting tides of history and politics. To explore the significance of the gold sovereigns was to embark on a journey through centuries of wealth, ambition, and treachery. The trail led us to shadowed corners of clandestine meetings, where deals were struck and fates decided in hushed tones. Every glint of the coin whispered tales of conquests and alliances, betrayals and noble sacrifices. The slow-burn suspense of our investigation mirrored the intricate dance of power and deception that characterized each era of the sovereigns' existence. The immensity of these gleaming treasures held an undeniable allure, beckoning us deeper into the labyrinth of their storied past. As we delved into the historical context surrounding these coins, we uncovered their unique role as both currency and emblems of authority. They stood at the nexus of trade and politics, shaping the destinies of nations and fueling the ambitions of rulers. The genuine gritty realism of our pursuit laid bare the raw emotions and harsh realities that underpinned the quest for these precious artifacts. Entwined with the fate of empires, the sovereigns carried within them the weight of dynasties risen and fallen, leaving enduring echoes across time. Navigate the winding trails of intrigue and avarice, we followed the golden thread of sovereignty, braving the shadows of looming conspiracies and the glint of treacherous ambition. The immersive historical detail brought to life the moments when these coins changed hands, each transaction laced with tension and peril. In our relentless pursuit, we unraveled the tangled web of allegiances and hostilities, woven tightly around every gleaming treasure. Ultimately, our relentless pursuit leads us through seedy

alleyways and opulent palaces alike, illuminating the dual nature of these golden artifacts: both instruments of power and silent witnesses to the rise and fall of civilizations. Thus, our exploration of the gold sovereigns' trail cast a piercing light on the enduring legacy of wealth, greed, and legacy that glittered through the annals of time.

Echoes in the Mint: Uncovering Hidden Stories

The echoes of history reverberate through the dimly lit chambers of the royal mint. As I navigated through the labyrinthine corridors, the scent of metal and ink hung heavy in the air, mingling with the palpable tension that seemed to permeate every brick and mortar. The mint was a place of secrets, where the clinking of coins masked the whispers of intrigue and power struggles that lay hidden beneath the surface. It was here, amid the rhythmic thud of the stamping presses, that the fate of nations was forged in precious metal. I sought out the custodian of the mint, a grizzled veteran who had witnessed decades of turbulent politics and shifting allegiances. In his weathered hands, he held the keys to the past, unlocking the stories that were buried within the engravings of each coin. His eyes held a world-weary wisdom, hinting at the countless narratives of ambition, betrayal, and redemption that had unfolded within these hallowed walls. As he spoke, the history of each sovereign came to life, woven with tales of treachery and triumph, of monarchs and rebels, and the relentless pursuit of power. Amongst the gleaming crucibles and towering stacks of bullion, I stumbled upon a forgotten alcove, its ancient shelves lined with dusty ledgers and faded parchments. Here, in this forgotten archive, lay the untold stories of forgery and deception, of desperate plots and grand deceptions that had eluded the annals of official history. The fragile pages yielded their secrets reluctantly, revealing a web of shadowy figures and clandestine operations that had shaped the very fabric of the kingdom. As night descended over the city, the mint took on an eerie aura of secrecy and foreboding. Whispers of long-buried scandals and forbidden affairs intertwined with the clatter of machinery, casting a cloak of uncertainty over my quest for the truth. Every muted footstep echoed in the empty corridors, heightening the sense of isolation and vulnerability. The weight of the unknown bore down upon me, urging me to unravel the enigma of the numismatic trail before it slipped through my fingers like grains of sand. In the depths of the mint, I unearthed a trove of enigmatic artifacts—hidden chambers, concealed compartments, and cryptic markings etched into the most coveted treasures. Here, amidst the relics of antiquity, lay the faint traces of a conspiracy that transcended time and borders. The cold touch of metal sent shivers down my spine as I pieced together the fragments of a puzzle that promised to illuminate the darkest corners of the past, while simultaneously plunging me deeper into a labyrinth of danger and deceit.

Currency and Power: A Fortune's Dangerous Path

The numismatic trail led deep into the heart of Tudor intrigue, where treacherous currents swirled around each glittering gold coin. Those who sought to possess these gleaming treasures risked more than mere wealth; they courted danger, power, and betrayal in equal measure. As our protagonists delved deeper into the folds of history, the shadows of greed and ambition loomed large, casting a grim and ominous pall over their noble quest. In the intriguing world of currency and power, fortunes were not forged from metal alone, but from the alliances and rivalries that underpinned the volatile Tudor court. Each golden sovereign bore witness to clandestine dealings, shifting loyalties, and deadly gambits, revealing a world where a single coin held the potential to shape destinies and alter the course of history itself. With every step along this dangerous path, our protagonists found themselves ensnared within a web of secrecy and peril. The mint, once believed to be a sanctuary of stability and order, whispered secrets of duplicity and manipulation. What appeared as mere coinage revealed itself as a pawn in the intricate game of power, exchanged as easily as a favor or a life. The allure of wealth and influence proved to be a siren's call, luring both the virtuous and the cunning into its irresistible grasp, each propelled by their own insatiable desires for supremacy. As they unearthed the true nature of this treacherous journey, the very foundation of their convictions trembled. What started as an innocent pursuit of historical artifacts now beckoned them toward a darker truth – one that threatened not just their own lives, but the fragile balance that held the kingdom together. The numismatic trail, once thought to be a beacon of enlightenment, now unveiled an unsettling reality, where power and wealth could corrupt even the noblest hearts and lead them down a perilous path towards an uncertain fate.

A Deadly Encounter: The Assassination Attempt Unfurls

The Gathering Storm: Tensions in the Courtyard
A humid afternoon sets the backdrop; whispers of unrest ripple through the palace as clandestine meetings take place under watchful eyes. The air is heavy with tension, tainted by the undercurrent of suspicion that courses through the courtyard. Courtiers exchange guarded glances, their measured steps betraying an underlying unease. The usual hum of activities is subdued, replaced by a palpable sense of anticipation tinged with dread. Each rustle of silk and hushed conversation adds to the mounting pressure, culminating in a simmering atmosphere that threatens to erupt at any moment. Shadows lengthen across the cobblestones, casting an ominous veil over the gathering, intensifying the sense of impending peril. As the day wanes, the sullen sky above mirrors the turbulent state of affairs within the palace walls, creating an eerie ambience that unnerves even the most seasoned inhabitants. The sensation of foreboding weighs heavily on the hearts of the courtiers, like a premonition of calamity lurking just beyond the confines of their sanctuary. It is in this charged atmosphere that the stage is set for the revelation of concealed motives and the unfolding of treacherous schemes, each thread of suspense pulling taut as the narrative hurtles towards its fateful climax.

Gleam of the Blade: Shadows and Intentions Revealed
As the dusk settled over the ancient castle, the flickering torchlight cast elongated shadows against the stone walls, adding an eerie sense of foreboding to the air. The tension that had been brewing within the courtyard now reached its crescendo, as whispered conversations and furtive glances gave way to a palpable sense of unease. Amidst the encroaching darkness, the gleam of a blade caught the light, momentarily illuminating the face of the figure brandishing it. Lurking in the periphery, their intentions remained shrouded in mystery, yet the sharp glint off the finely honed steel hinted at a resolve tempered by danger. In the dimly lit corners of the courtyard, subtle movements betrayed

the presence of hidden watchers, their eyes trained on the unfolding drama. The suspense hung heavy in the air, weaving a tangled web of uncertainty that seemed to seep into every crevice. With each heartbeat, the anticipation swelled, echoing through the fraught silence as the weight of impending peril settled like a heavy cloak upon the assembled courtiers. For within the dance of shifting shadows, intentions were laid bare in the clandestine exchange between adversaries, a silent duel played out amidst the gathering gloom. The murmur of betrayal lingered, intertwined with the whispers of long-held grievances and unspoken threats. Every gesture, every lingering gaze spoke volumes, revealing the intricacies of loyalty and deceit that had woven themselves into the very fabric of courtly life. Against the backdrop of political intrigue and simmering animosity, the gleam of the blade served as a stark reminder of the perilous dance embarked upon by those entangled in the machinations of power. The glint of steel held captive the reflection of unspoken truths, casting a chilling light on the clandestine underworld that churned beneath the facade of regal opulence. In this singular moment, the revelation of shadowed intentions lent a chilling clarity to the complex interplay of ambition and treachery, plunging the gathering into the heart of a gripping narrative spun from the tapestry of history itself.

The Fractured Hour: Fate Meets Desperation

As the moon hung low in the ink-black sky, a hushed tension gripped the opulent chambers of the Tudor court. The air was heavy with the unmistakable aroma of intrigue and the palpable weight of impending catastrophe. Within the flickering candlelight, figures moved like wraiths, their breath catching in their throats as they exchanged furtive glances and urgent whispers. This fractured hour bore witness to an intricate dance of fate and desperation, where every shadow concealed peril and every silence held the echo of treachery. Caught in the unyielding grip of uncertainty, the courtiers' faces betrayed the strain of hidden agendas and unspoken alliances. Against this backdrop of murky intentions and seditious undertones, a lone figure emerged from the gloom, bearing the burden of both duty and defiance. The harsh lines of his countenance spoke volumes of the trials he had endured, the sacrifices made in service to crown and conscience. Across the chamber, a sudden gust of wind stirred the heavy damask curtains, casting a spectral pall over the assembled company. In that fleeting moment, time seemed to fracture, every heartbeat reverberating with the merciless march towards an inevitable reckoning. Amidst this tapestry of anticipation and deceit, a tremor ran through the room as the steady rhythm of footsteps heralded the approach of destiny's hand. Each footfall rang out like a thunderous proclamation, as if the very ground beneath quaked in recognition of the impending tumult. At the heart of the chamber, a glint of steel caught the dim light, casting an ethereal sheen that mesmerized and forewarned in equal measure. Eyes widened in fearful recognition as the cruel reality of the hour unfurled, revealing the fatal convergence of malevolence and resolve. In the fractured hour, fate met desperation with a chilling inevitability, entwining the destinies of those present in an unbreakable coil of peril and sacrifice. The imperceptible shift of power hung heavy in the air, a promise of cataclysmic upheaval that would rend the fragile fabric of the Tudor court asunder.

Behind Closed Doors: Secrets of the Queen's Privy Chambers

Whispers Amid the Tapestry: Unspoken Anxieties of the Court
The court, with its opulent chambers and intricate tapestries, is a microcosm of intrigue and hidden tensions. The air hangs heavy with unspoken anxieties as courtiers skillfully dance through the delicate web of politics and power. Every word uttered and every glance exchanged carries layers of unspoken meanings and concealed agendas. The tension is palpable, like a tightly wound thread ready to unravel at the slightest provocation. In the flickering candlelight, whispered conversations take on an air of secrecy, their hushed tones hinting at clandestine alliances and treacherous schemes. The guarded looks and surreptitious glances reveal the underlying unease that permeates the court, where loyalties are as fragile as the fragile threads of silk woven into the exquisite tapestries that adorn the walls. Each courtier moves with calculated steps, their every action a carefully choreographed dance to maintain their precarious positions in the intricate hierarchy of influence and power. As the faint strains of music echo through the halls, the atmosphere becomes even more charged, as if the very notes themselves carry the weight of whispered confidences and unspoken fears. Behind the façade of splendor and grandeur, the court pulses with an undercurrent of apprehension, as those within its gilded confines navigate the treacherous waters of politics and ambition. Each painted smile and gracious nod conceals a multitude of fears and ambitions, as allegiances shift like shadows cast by the flickering torchlight. Amidst the ornate surroundings and the ostentatious displays of wealth, there exists a gritty realism that underscores the slow-burn suspense of courtly life. In this world of intricate subterfuge and covert maneuvering, the immersive historical detail captures the essence of a volatile era where alliances are forged and shattered behind closed doors, where whispers can topple empires and unspoken anxieties hold the key to survival in the perilous game of courtly politics.
Reflective Gaze: Deciphering Clues in the Royal Sanctuary

The royal sanctuary loomed with an air of opulence and secrecy as we ventured through its corridors, lined with priceless tapestries and flickering torches that cast eerie shadows. Every footstep seemed to echo the weight of history, each creak of the floorboards a reminder of the intrigue that permeated the queen's inner sanctum. As we approached her private chambers, a hush fell upon our group, the silence heavy with the unspoken tensions of courtly life. The anticipation was palpable, hanging in the air like a cloud of secrets waiting to be revealed. Upon entering the queen's sanctuary, one could not help but be struck by the ornate furnishings and elaborate decor that whispered of wealth and power. Yet beneath the surface glamour lay subtle clues—carefully positioned objects, cryptic symbols, and hidden compartments—that hinted at a deeper layer of clandestine activity. It was as if the very walls held their breath, drawing us into a world of shadowy whispers and elusive mysteries. With every careful glance and hesitant touch, we sought to unravel the enigma that shrouded the queen's true intentions. The slow-burn suspense was all-consuming, each small detail scrutinized and analyzed for its potential significance. In the dim candlelight, time seemed to stretch endlessly as we pieced together the fragments of a puzzle centuries in the making, our senses attuned to every nuance and subtlety. Immersed in the historical detail of the regal surroundings, we delved into the intricate web of codes and symbols that adorned the chamber. Each piece of furniture, each painting, and every seemingly innocent trinket held the potential to unlock a trove of secrets, serving as a testament to the gritty realism of courtly life. The tension continued to build, mirroring the undercurrent of political unrest that simmered just beneath the veneer of grandeur. As we gazed upon the meticulously arranged artifacts, the weight of historical significance pressed in upon us, compelling us to dig deeper into the queen's private intrigues. The reflective gaze cast upon the room's rich tapestries and gilded artifacts offered a window into the turbulent times of Tudor England, shedding light on the hidden machinations that shaped the course of history.
Hidden Alcoves and Secret Correspondence: The Queen's Private Intrigues

The labyrinthine corridors of the royal chambers held more than just opulent tapestries and gilded decorations. Nestled within the deep recesses of the Queen's private alcoves were whispers of clandestine meetings and covert exchanges, shielded from the prying eyes of the courtiers. As I ventured through these dimly lit passages, a sense of trepidation washed over me, knowing that every step brought me closer to unraveling the enigma that lay veiled in the shadows. At the heart of the alcove, a small escritoire stood like a sentinel, its mahogany surface adorned with delicate carvings of roses and thorns, mirroring the intricate web of alliances and intrigues that encircled the Queen's court. With trembling hands, I traced the patterns etched into the wood, an unsettling reminder of the thorny path that lay ahead in uncovering the secrets concealed within. The flickering candlelight cast dancing shadows upon a pile of parchment, revealing snippets of cryptic missives exchanged between the Queen and her trusted confidantes. Each word seemed to emanate an aura of palpable tension, pregnant with unspoken implications and veiled agendas. It was evident that within these innocuous sheets of paper lay the threads that connected the disparate players in this elaborate game of power and subterfuge. As I pored over the clandestine correspondence, the slow-burn suspense of the Queen's private intrigues began to unfold before my eyes. The ink-stained pages bore witness to a world steeped in gritty realism, where loyalties wavered and allegiances were as fickle as the shifting tides. Amidst the meticulously penned lines, I discerned subtle hints of a web of deceit woven with calculated precision, designed to ensnare those who dared challenge the Queen's authority. The chamber exuded an immersive historical detail, evoking the bygone era with its hushed whispers and palpable undercurrents of political machinations. Every crevice harbored echoes of secrets that had long remained veiled from prying eyes, shrouded in the mists of time and guarded by the unwavering silence of the tapestries that adorned the walls. In the Queen's private domain, the air itself seemed to vibrate with the weight of untold secrets, each one a cog in the intricate machinery of courtly intrigue. And as the shadows lengthened and the candle flames flickered in their sconces, I braced myself for the revelations that lay dormant within the hidden alcoves, poised to reshape the course of history with their whispered truths.

Code of Silence: Testing Loyalties and Intentions

A Whisper in the Dark: Loyal Servants or Secret Betrayers?
The tension within the dimly lit halls of the court was palpable, suffocating even the most loyal with doubt. Clandestine meetings occurred in the shadows, the faces of attendees betraying the gravity of their conversations. Trusted confidants exchanged furtive glances, their professed loyalty at odds with the whispers that echoed in the chamber. The slow-burn suspense of treachery simmered beneath the carefully constructed facades of allegiance, secrets threatening to spill into the open like poison from a hidden vial. As intercepted messages became an inherent part of the web of trust and suspicion, their content became the linchpin on which loyalties teetered. Each parchment held the potential to either reinforce bonds of alliance or unravel the fragile ties that bound courtiers together. The immersive historical detail underscored the weight carried by each intercepted correspondence, the intricacies of language and code mirroring the complexities of the political landscape where trust was a precious commodity. In the midst of this labyrinth of intrigue, a servant stumbled upon a hidden cache of messages, their contents as volatile as wildfire in the royal court. The accidental discovery sparked turmoil within the once unyielding bastions of loyalty, igniting internal conflict and laying bare the fault lines of deception that ran deep within the heart of the court. The gritty realism of this revelation cast a harsh light on the illusion of unity, chipping away at the veneer of camaraderie to unveil the stark reality of duplicity and self-interest. The realization dawned that every murmured conversation, every seemingly obedient gesture had been tainted by the clandestine dealings that operated just beneath the surface. It was a startling revelation that threatened to erode the very foundation of trust, leaving courtiers grappling with the realization that those whom they had once considered steadfast allies might harbor motives veiled in shadows. This chapter in the tale of palace intrigue highlighted the immutable forces that drove individuals to preserve their own standing, even

at the cost of sowing discord among the tightly woven fabric of loyalty.

The Test of Faith: Under Shadows' Watchful Eyes

The air hung heavy with the scent of incense and apprehension as the flickering flames of the candles cast wavering shadows on the stone walls. The chamber was cloaked in an eerie hush, broken only by the distant sounds of muffled footsteps and whispered conversations. Every person present seemed to be holding their breath, their eyes flitting nervously around the room, searching for any sign of treachery. For weeks, rumors had been swirling through the court, weaving a web of suspicion around the most trusted advisors of the queen. Loyalties were questioned, and allegiances tested in the quiet confines of this dimly lit chamber. Each individual present knew that their every move was being scrutinized, their every word weighed for hidden meaning. As the tension mounted, subtle cues of authority emerged within the shifting shadows, the air ripe with distrust and uncertainty. The flicker of a raised eyebrow, the clenching of a jaw, the avoidance of eye contact – all seemingly innocuous actions, yet pregnant with unspoken significance. It became apparent that everyone present was engaged in a complex dance of deception and distrust, where even the slightest misstep could lead to dire consequences. In the midst of this suffocating atmosphere, loyalties that had once seemed unwavering now trembled under the weight of suspicion. Friends cast furtive glances at one another, questioning the motives behind each fleeting expression, each fleeting gesture. The bonds of trust, painstakingly built over years of service, threatened to unravel under the strain of doubt and fear. Even the flickering candlelight seemed to conspire against them, casting elongated shadows that distorted familiar features into grotesque masks of uncertainty. Each face held a story, a secret, a lie waiting to be uncovered. And as the minutes stretched into hours, the silence grew thicker, punctuated only by the racing heartbeat of each participant, reflecting the palpable anxiety that hung in the air. The weight of duty and allegiance pressed down on every soul in the chamber, entwining their fates in a tangled skein of intrigue and danger. No one could escape the merciless scrutiny that permeated the clandestine meeting, nor the chilling realization that in the game of loyalty, trust was a luxury none could afford. The test of faith had begun, and each individual found themselves teetering on the razor's edge of perilous consequences, their destinies hanging in the balance.

Crossroads of Trust: Decisions in the Candle-lit Night

The candle-lit night enveloped the clandestine meeting, casting long shadows across the dimly lit chamber. Each flickering flame seemed to hold its breath as the air hung heavy with the weight of unspoken secrets. The silence was punctuated only by the occasional whisper and the creak of an old wooden floorboard underfoot. At the center of the room, figures stood cloaked in darkened attire, their faces obscured by the dancing interplay of light and darkness. This gathering had been carefully orchestrated, bringing together individuals whose allegiances lay hidden beneath layers of calculated indifference. The subtle tension in the air hinted at the precarious nature of the alliances that bound these shadowy conspirators together. As the night wore on, the conversation ebbed and flowed like the tide, weaving a web of words that masked true intentions and motivations. Each participant navigated the treacherous terrain of half-truths and elusive promises, testing the limits of trust and loyalty. Every carefully chosen phrase held the potential to unravel carefully constructed facades, exposing the raw vulnerabilities that lay beneath. Amidst this intricate dance of deceit, the candlelight seemed to flicker with a life of its own, casting uncertain glimmers of hope and doubt upon the faces of those gathered. Suspicion hung thick in the air, intertwining with the heady scent of intrigue and apprehension. In the midst of this fragile equilibrium, pivotal decisions loomed like unseen specters in the night. The weight of consequence bore down upon each participant, forcing them to navigate the perilous crossroads of trust and betrayal. Whispers of treachery brushed against the edges of possibility, threatening to shatter the delicate balance that held this clandestine assembly together. Yet, amidst the cloak-and-dagger machinations, the echoes of shared history and common cause pulsed quietly beneath the surface. A tentative thread of unity wove its way through the tangled web of suspicion and doubt, binding these disparate individuals together in a fragile alliance borne of necessity. As the candle-lit night drew to a close, the participants faced the harrowing choice of whether to embrace the shadows of distrust or to grasp the flickering embers of solidarity. The outcome of their deliberations would send ripples through the intricate tapestry of courtly intrigue, shaping the fate of kingdoms and destinies alike.

The Brink of War: A Kingdom in Balance

Gathering Storm: Diplomatic Tensions and Political Maneuvers
As diplomats move in shadows, secret meetings and whispered strategies heighten tension between rival factions. It was a time of delicate balance, with every word spoken, every alliance forged, shaping the destiny of the kingdom. In the dimly lit chambers of court, envoys from foreign lands engaged in subtle dances of negotiation, their expressions carefully guarded as they sought to gain the upper hand without revealing their true intentions. The air crackled with anticipation, each diplomatic encounter a potential precursor to either peace or chaos. Amidst the veneer of civility, alliances were tested and betrayals plotted behind closed doors, where loyalties were as fragile as parchment in a rainstorm. Every move, every gesture held the weight of a nation's future. Across the map, political maneuvering mirrored the shifting sands of power, as whispers of treaties and secret pacts carried the promise of security or the threat of impending conflict. The stakes could not be higher as the web of allegiances tightened, weaving a complex tapestry of uncertainty. In this tangled web, even the most seasoned diplomats found themselves ensnared, forced to navigate treacherous waters in pursuit of elusive stability. Meanwhile, at the fringes of society, rumors swirled like eddies in a river, carrying tales of unspoken agreements and veiled threats. Each development, no matter how minor, resonated through the corridors of power, igniting sparks that threatened to engulf the entire realm. As the days grew shorter and tensions mounted, the kingdom teetered on the brink of upheaval, caught in the grip of a relentless storm brewing on the horizon. Diplomatic tension had never been so palpable, nor the specter of war so imminent. With every passing day, the gathering storm cast a long shadow over the fate of all who called this kingdom home.
Rumblings from the Front: Soldiers Prepare for Uncertainty
The soldiers march with a weary determination, their footsteps echoing in the mist-shrouded dawn. Each man carries the weight of uncertainty on his shoulders, knowing that the rumblings of war draw ever closer. Their faces are etched with grim resolve,

yet their eyes betray the flicker of fear that dances on the edge of their consciousness. It is in these quiet moments before the storm that the true mettle of a soldier is tested. With each passing day, the tension mounts within the camp, as whispers of impending conflict ripple through the ranks. Every clank of armor and sharpening of blades serves as a somber symphony, a prelude to the violence that looms on the horizon. The air crackles with palpable unease, as men steal moments of solitude to pen farewell missives or seek solace in silent prayer. Amidst the pervasive sense of foreboding, bonds forged in battle grow stronger, offering a lifeline of camaraderie amidst the encroaching darkness. These soldiers, molded by the harsh embrace of duty, find solace in the shared burden of preparedness. Hardened veterans impart their wisdom to fresh-faced recruits, instilling in them the gravity of the task at hand. Each day brings new drills, the rhythmic thud of swords against shields resounding across the training grounds. The sun sets upon weary silhouettes, the waning light casting elongated shadows that seem to embrace the imminent unknown. At night, dreams are plagued by visions of conflict, while whispered conversations drift like smoke above the campfires, mulling over strategies and recounting battles fought in distant lands. The slow-burn suspense tightens its grasp upon the soldiers, shaping them into a cohesive force ready to face the impending tempest. As the anticipatory tension reaches its zenith, the soldiers stand on the precipice of uncertainty, their resolve tempered by the unforgiving reality of war's imminent arrival.

Final Stratagems: Calculated Risks in the Shadow of Conflict

Amid the rolling hills and dense woodlands, the commanders surveyed their troops with unyielding resolve etched upon their weathered faces. The air crackled with trepidation as soldiers sharpened their blades and adjusted their armor, preparing for the imminent clash that threatened to plunge the kingdom into chaos. Scouts rode in with reports of enemy movements, their apprehensive whispers hinting at the looming confrontation beyond the horizon. Every strategy was scrutinized, every resource meticulously allocated, as the fate of the realm hung precariously in the balance. On the eve of battle, the commanders convened in a secluded tent, their grim expressions illuminated by flickering torchlight. Tense discussions unfolded, punctuated by urgent deliberations on tactics and contingencies. The weight of responsibility bore heavily upon them, shrouded beneath layers of stoic composure. Each decision held the potential to sway the tides of war—the calculated risks measured against the backdrop of an uncertain future. At dawn, the soldiers assembled in disciplined ranks, their banners billowing amidst the chill morning breeze. The tension was palpable, a silent anticipation that gripped the hearts of those poised to march towards the crucible of conflict. As they advanced, the landscape transformed into a theatre of war—a mire of tumultuous emotions interwoven with the vivid tapestry of historical significance. The clash was relentless, marked by the deafening clang of steel meeting steel and the anguished cries of the fallen. The gritty realism of combat left no room for romanticized notions, painting a visceral tableau of human struggle amidst the brutality of armed conflict. The slow-burn suspense of each skirmish unfurled like a tautly wound thread, weaving a narrative of uncertainty and peril. Amidst the ebb and flow of battle, the immersive historical detail spoke volumes of the sacrifices made and the unwavering resolve that echoed through the annals of time. As the sun dipped below the bloodied horizon, the echoes of conflict gradually waned. The aftermath bore witness to the toll exacted by warfare, as the wounded were tended to and the fallen honored with somber reverence. Despite the ferocity of battle, the kingdom stood—its delicate balance upheld by the steadfast courage and unwavering determination of those who braved the crucible of war. Their sacrifice would be etched into the annals of history, a testament to the indomitable spirit that prevailed in the face of adversity.

Printed in Dunstable, United Kingdom

79068340R00037